THE WEIRS

A Winnipesaukee Adventure

To Harlow,
May all your good fortunes come true!
Best Wishes,
Andy Opel

by Andy Opel

Illustrated by Karel Hayes & John Gorey

Jetty House • Portsmouth, NH

Dedicated to
Jane Rainie Opel
and the power of mother-son collaboration

and

To friends and family who have been or hope to be visitors to the lake. - KH

The Loon Center in Moultonborough, New Hampshire is home to the Loon Preservation Committee (LPC) and the Frederick and Paula Anna Markus Wildlife Sanctuary. The Center is the perfect destination to learn about loons and LPC's work to preserve loons and their habitats throughout New Hampshire. Educational displays, award-winning videos, a nature store and hiking trails are among the Loon Center's attractions.
For more information visit: www.loon.org.

The Loon Preservation Committee was created in 1975 in response to a dramatic decline in New Hampshire's loon population and the effects of human activities on loons. It is LPC's mission to restore and maintain a healthy population of loons throughout New Hampshire; to monitor the health and productivity of loon populations as sentinels of environmental quality; and to promote a greater understanding of loons and the larger natural world.

Graphic design by Charity Myers www.thecreativepooldesign.com

Printed in the USA
ISBN13: 978-1-937721-12-1
Library of Congress Control Number: 2013934632

Published by
Jetty House
an imprint of
Peter E. Randall Publisher
Box 4726, Portsmouth, NH 03802
www.perpublisher.com

www.lakewinniadventures.com

Every summer, Jack, Franny and J.J. would come
to visit their grandmother at Lake Winnipesaukee.

They all shared a special bedroom in Boulder Lodge, the cottage by the lake. "I love the sound of the lake waking me up in the morning," Franny said.

"I like the patterns of light the morning sun makes on the ceiling," added Jack.

"I like the sound the loons make—then I know summer is here and my grandchildren will be coming to visit," said Grammy as she helped the kids get settled.

One thing all three children looked forward to was when
Mr. Fuller would take them to The Weirs in his boat.
"I want to sit next to Grammy," said J.J.

"Me too," said Franny.

"Jack, why don't you sit in the front with me?" said Mr. Fuller.

Mr. Fuller liked to take the long way to The Weirs,
and he always went fast as they crossed The Broads.

"Look, there is the *Sophie C.* delivering mail to Jolly Island," said Grammy.

"Do they deliver food too?" asked J.J., wondering about the people on the island.

"No, they have to take a boat to shore when they go to the store," said Grammy.

"I have a surprise I want to show you." said Mr. Fuller.

"I hope it's not The Witches," said J.J. "I still don't like witches."

"This is something special, but we need to be very quiet,"
said Mr. Fuller as he slowed the boat down to idle speed and passed
through the narrow channel between Mink Island and Mark Island.

"Look closely everyone," said Mr. Fuller. "That is a loon, and she has a baby
riding on her back." Mr. Fuller let the boat come to a stop as they all quietly
watched the mother loon swim across the channel.

"That's cool," said Jack. "I've never seen a baby loon before."

"They are rare birds, and we are lucky to have them on the lake," said Mr. Fuller.

"Why don't you take a turn at the wheel Jack?" Mr. Fuller said.
Jack gave a big smile as he moved behind the wheel.
Jack made the boat go fast, and Grammy spread out her arms and yelled,
"We can fly, we can fly!" They all laughed as the wind blew their hair
and water gently splashed their faces.

As they came around Governor's Island, they could see the boardwalk and the arcades. "There's The Weirs," said Grammy.

"I want to play Skee-ball," said Franny.

"I want to play pinball," said Jack.

"Yeah, me too," said J.J.

Walking into the arcade, they saw an old fortune teller machine.
"Look J.J., a fortune teller," said Franny. "It says, 'What does Grandma say?'"

"She's not a real Grandma like you, Grammy, is she?" asked J.J.
"I don't like that old witch lady."

"She's not a witch; she's a fortune teller," said Jack. "Go ahead, make a wish; she might bring you good luck."

"Why don't you let her tell your fortune?" said Grammy as she handed J.J. a coin.

J.J. put the coin in the machine and the fortune teller came to life, breathing slowly, moving her hand over her playing cards and looking at J.J. with her glass eyes. J.J. stepped back and hid behind Grammy's leg. A card came out of the slot at the bottom of the machine and the fortune teller went back to sleep.
"What does it say, Grammy?" asked J.J., picking up the card.

Grammy read the card: "Stars will fall from the sky and your wishes will come true."

"That's weird," said J.J. "I hope the stars don't fall on me."

The children all played games.
"I won a free game of pinball," said Jack.

"J.J. and I won 20 tickets playing Skee-ball," said Franny.

"I want to get that toy sailboat with the tickets," said J.J.

"The sailboat is 50 tickets J.J.; we don't have nearly enough," said Franny.

"I never win the prize," said J.J., disappointed that he could not get the toy boat.

While the children were getting ice cream with Mr. Fuller, Grammy went back to play just a little more Skee-ball. Her years of practice made getting high scores and lots of tickets as easy as jumping off the dock.

"Come on, everyone; it is getting dark," said Mr. Fuller.

As they climbed into the boat, J.J. got a blanket and snuggled up to Grammy in the back seat.

"Look at all the lights," said Franny as they moved out into Weirs Bay. Many boats were anchored in the bay and their red and green bow lights sparkled off the water. Mr. Fuller turned the motor off and let the boat drift just as a loud boom came from the shore.

"Fireworks!" exclaimed Jack as a huge blossom of color burst in the sky.

"Oooohhh," said Franny.

"Aaahhhh," said J.J.

"Look at that one, J.J.," said Jack. "It's just like the fortune teller said, 'stars falling from the sky.'"

"But my wish didn't come true because I wanted that sailboat," said J.J.

Just then, Grammy pulled the toy sailboat out of her bag and handed it to J.J.
His eyes got big and a smile spread across his face.
"The fortune teller was right!" exclaimed J.J.

"Your Grammy is an old pro at Skee-ball," said Mr. Fuller.
"And she knows how to make your wishes come true."

The children all nodded in agreement.
"And now it's time to go home," said Mr. Fuller, as he slowly
steered the boat out of the crowded bay.

Mr. Fuller followed the silvery path from the moon as they drove back to the cottage. All three children fell asleep in the boat before they got home to the dock.

The End